Joining
the
Choir
Invisible

The following is an exclusive imprint of Summer House Publishing

and Summer House Media LLC

www.summerhousepublishing.co

www.jdwritesbooks.com

For rights, literary requests or other inquiries, please contact Chris Varonos at: chris@summerhousemedia.co

Edited by Christine Nielson

Cover and interior design by Nuno Moreira, NM DESIGN

ISBN: 978-1-7372920-0-5

Joining the Choir Invisible

a story by

JD SLAJCHERT

To Whiskey Joe. See you when I see you.

OTHER STORIES

MoonFlower

Open Curtains:

Good morning, good afternoon or good evening, ladies and gentlemen, and welcome to *Joining the Choir Invisible*. Wherever this story finds you, we are thrilled you could make it. As not to distract the performers and for your own personal viewing enjoyment, please note that any use of Instagram, Facebook, Twitter, Snapchat or Tik Tok during our performance is strictly prohibited. This is a reminder for you and those around you that all mobile phones should also be turned off, not on silent. Should you be required to use your mobile phone, or any social media whatsoever, we suggest that you please stop reading and pick up again from the beginning at a later time when convenient for you. Thank you, and we greatly appreciate your cooperation.

Now, please find your seats as we are all set to begin. We hope you enjoy the show.

It cannot be that there is life after death. It cannot be that we are judged by some man in the sky. It cannot be that He either chooses to beam down voices of reason or He chooses to strike down lightning of sin. There is no fairness in life, so there must be no fairness in any existence of an after. In youth, we find warmth in a place beyond the clouds, yet in age there is no such warmth. With age comes only the desire to shield those unknown. But once that is lost, then all is lost. We are protectors, or better even, we are storytellers. We are storytellers tasked with perpetuating the falsehood of an after, knowing full well that no such fairytale exists. There is only here, now, today. A short moment that eventually, like all other moments, runs out of life to burn.

I took my eyes from the snowstorm outside the parlor back to the Old Man beside me. It was like every other parlor I'd been in, fingerprinted drinking glasses and aged wood beams. Behind the Old Man was the boy, a young bartender with only a smattering of hair on his fresh face.

My eyes stuck with the Old Man and I wondered then not if, but when he'd broken. If not for his breaks, I knew I wouldn't find him beside me now.

"Why do you drink?" I asked, my fingers tracing the letters on the bottle of Jameson he'd insisted the bartender leave with me. The Old Man had his own bottle of gin. It was the kind of move that let me know we'd stay awhile.

But the Old Man was now the one with his attention out the window. My eyes followed his. The trees appeared to be on stilts. Almost like matches. Long, thin matches that pushed them past the storm. They were so thin they appeared frail. But because of their towering height, they did not need to concern themselves with the below. Too high up to worry about the small specs of life.

Hundreds of those trees stood over us in the cabin. Even despite the blustering storm, their stillness was eerie. Like matches still, or even statues, they just watched us. Judged us, standing tall above all of that smothering, percolating snow. Waiting for the storm to stop so they could ignite.

With phlegm in the back of his chapped throat, the Old Man answered in his Canadian twang. "To get to my love again sooner, bud. Hard to see much of a point in any of this without her. But, also, for the conversation...for the truths unlocked in every man beyond each sip. *In vino veritas*. A closer look, ya know, Don?"

My hands were now both atop the table. The scarred wood felt worn beneath my fingertips. All of the different hands and glasses and bottles it must have seen. All of the different dialogues it must have witnessed.

The Old Man wore a gold wedding band, the glint of the bar lights showing off its dings and nicks.

"Where would you see her?" I asked, fiddling with my naked ring finger.

"In the after," the Old Man began. "I've been a God-fearing Christian my entire life. Her, too, bud. I'll be seeing her again. I'm certain."

An ache went through my leg then. I poked around for my prescription in my pocket but settled for my drink instead.

"Life here...that's the only thing you can be certain about," I said, slipping my hand back out of my pocket.

The Old Man laughed a deep, low laugh. One that let me know I hadn't shaken his constitution one bit.

"Without her, there is no *here*, ya know?" The Old Man took a quick sip of his gin. "I'll be seeing her again, Don. Don't you worry, bud, I'll be seeing her again."

The Old Man reached into his pocket and handed me a photo. It was in black and white. She looked special. Her eyes were lively, and her cheeks appeared as though they'd been accustomed to smiling frequently. Someone you'd notice.

"We built this old thing together." He waved, indicating the cabin. "Our families both grew up cottaging around here. Sometimes in the summers, but mostly winters. The lake isn't too far...we've met some pretty great folks through all our time here, bud. It's...it's intimate, ya know. The way you get to know people. Not too much else to distract you, bud. Not too much else."

My eyes left the photo and went back to the rest of the cabin. The long logs that stabilized the structure. The tawny sofa near the front door. I could see more photos of her and the Old Man on the other walls. Photos of them with just one another and photos of them with others.

"She could really entertain, ya know. You'd have liked her Don. Seriously, bud, you would have. Real charmer, and she was super smart. Much smarter than me."

"Kids?"

The Old Man then lost some of his pep. "She'd always wanted 'em, but we weren't so fortunate. It's a terrible thing because she would've been a fine mom. I'm not so sure about me, ya know, but I think you become a dad over time. At least some dads do."

I adjusted my chair so my back wasn't as stiff. Most of the things in here were old, but the chair could at least do the trick.

"It's funny, ya know," the Old Man began. "I'd pined after her for years, yet she'd wanted nothing to do with me. When we'd been cottaging, I'd send her all sorts of things. Flowers, cards, chocolates. But none of that stuff worked. She could see right through it. Like I said, ya know, she was smart. She knew I was full of it, bud...she knew. But do you want to know what finally settled it?" The Old Man waited only half a breath before answering himself. "I grew up." The Old Man laughed. "Girls date boys, ya know, but women? Women only date men."

I was in my whiskey. Sucking on it like a bee to sweet clover. Listening to the aged gravel of the Old Man's voice.

"But that's the irony in getting old." The Old Man settled down. "You gain all this wisdom, yet you're past the time to use it."

The Old Man coughed again. It was full-bodied this time.

"I should've danced more with her, ya know. No...I should've taken her out dancing more. Let the world see her dance. Let the world see...her." The Old Man then snapped his fingers and swayed in his chair. "What about you then, bud?" the Old Man asked, his voice starting to slur as the liquor took hold.

I didn't say anything. I was starting to get more tired, anyway.

"You a God-fearing Christian, Don?"

A loud hiss slapped the walls of the cabin. Outside now, the storm was growing more violent. The wood around us shivered.

"I'm not sure that quite matters." I swirled the whiskey in my glass.

The Old Man snapped. "Of course it does! Either you believe or you don't, ya know. And it matters alright, Don. Trust me, bud, it matters."

My Jameson was going down like water now. I poured myself another couple fingers from the bottle. Some of it splashed onto the table.

"It doesn't matter what I think because there is no after," I said. "And even if there was, I wouldn't have anyone there anyway."

The Old Man tried to warm me back up. "Sure, you do. Good looking fella like you surely has a wife that one day will join you there. Parents, perhaps. I'm sure you've got a lot of people that will be waiting, ya know."

"Ex-wife," I corrected the Old Man before going for my freshly-poured whiskey. I could smell the malted grains on my own breath.

As the night wore on, the warmth from the bottle seeped into my tongue, jaw.

The Old Man prodded. "This ex-wife. She's…"

"In Moricetown. Once the storm passes, I'm taking my daughter there."

"Sweet, bud. Very sweet then." The Old Man patted the table. "And how long are ya visiting for?"

"How about we just drink, Old Man?" I growled. "I would just like to drink and watch the snow."

I didn't even bother to look at the Old Man. I was so fed up. He'd been pestering me far longer than I liked.

I looked down into my glass and tossed back the last of my Jameson. I tipped the bottle over the glass. Only a few drops. The bottle was empty.

"Another?" the Old Man asked.

"I'll get it." I set the empty glass on the table. "Could use the exercise."

Pulling my bad leg out from under the table, I dragged myself to the bar where the bartender was cleaning our dinner plates. He was young, his eyes were full. I could only see the hair on his cheeks and upper lip since I was standing right before him. He talked like the Old Man but with less of an accent.

I set my glass on the bar.

"More medicine?"

I pushed my glass forward as he reached for another bottle. "Another finger. Maybe two."

He unscrewed the lid and filled the glass halfway. I limped back to the table.

The Old Man pulled my chair out. I sat down and settled into the same slump I'd been in.

"Your daughter," the Old Man said between cracked teeth. "She's real sweet, Don. Real sweet, ya know."

I pushed my jacket up around my neck and nodded. I took a sip.

From behind me, the bartender scoffed. "I wouldn't pay it much mind though, sir. The Old Man here hardly ever sees anyone in the winter."

The previously mild-tempered Old Man exploded out of his chair, shooting to his feet so fast both of his knees made a popping noise. He slapped a hand on the bar top, his gin sloshing in the glass of his other and spit his words with ire at the bartender.

"Boy! You don't know the first thing about manners!

If I could run this cottage myself, you'd be on your stinking ass out in that cold, ya know!" the Old Man snarled while shaking his head. He chucked back the rest of his gin and slammed his glass on the bar top.

The Old Man violently coughed as it went down. His rutted beard caught some of the saliva that accumulated in the corners of his lips. With a frayed handkerchief, he wiped his cheeks, mouth.

The bartender gave the Old Man a subtle glare and then continued with his dishes.

"How is she? Your…"

"Squeeze." I said back to the Old Man as he settled down into his seat again. "Everyone just calls her Squeeze."

The Old Man smiled. "I thought I heard you calling her that when the two of ya checked in, bud. A lively soul. Just like her father."

I was now well into my drink and hoping only to become more so. I hadn't been expecting company.

"There are some great sights for the two of you in Smithers, ya know. Once the storm passes through." The Old Man coughed more deeply than the first time, his shoulders shaking with it.

The liquor on my lips helped them feel less dry. After driving all day, it was also pleasant to finally have graduated from bottled water. The leg space in my compact was absolute perdition.

"Yeah! Check out the looney bin up in Witset!" the

bartender yelled from the back. "I've only heard the rumors, but I'm sure they'll take great care of Squeeze if you're looking to get rid of her!"

"Boy!" The Old Man shot up and threw his gin right at the bartender. The spinning glass shot out of his hand like a bullet. It missed the bartender by a hair and if it hadn't it may have killed the kid. The glass shattered and hit a couple of bottles on the shelf. All of them spilled onto the floor like a running faucet.

The bartender started howling in laughter as the Old Man stood in a stance like an ace pitcher post fastball.

The Old Man then reached over the bar and started choking the bartender by his collar—pulling on his tie and vest.

With fire, he snarled, "Some fucking chops! You're swine! Swine! All you damn kids now are swine!"

As the two of them bickered, I slid behind the bar to pick up the broken glass. It's not that I wasn't angry, but more that I'd been through enough pain and didn't want to unleash more of it on anyone. I was simply tired.

The bartender's laughter slowed just as the Old Man ran out of breath and relaxed his grip.

"Get the fucking mop." The Old Man released the bartender's collar.

The bartender tugged his shirt into place as he disappeared into the back room.

The Old Man joined me as he wiped a bead of sweat off his oily forehead.

"Don't pay the boy any mind, bud. You'll stay for free on account of everything. It's truly the least I can do, ya know."

I kept picking up the glass until the Old Man stopped me.

"Don, you're bleeding."

I looked at my hand and saw I'd sliced my finger and wrist on my right hand. I hadn't even realized it.

The Old Man waved me away. "Here, don't worry about the rest. The kid will get it, eh. The kid will. Just go and sit down. Let me find something for that."

I went back to my seat and found the Jameson now with my left. In silence, I stared out the window again like before. The angle of all the snow. The soft stacking of powder that blanketed the layers before. The wind that carried all of them into one after the other after the other.

I sighed deeply as I reached again for my glass, only to find that it was empty.

"Don't worry, Don," the Old Man said as he returned to the table with the other bottle of Jameson. He set it down next to the first. "Now, let me see those cuts on your hand."

The Old Man gingerly took my finger in his as the blood carried on with its velvet drip. He patted it with a square of gauze, the white, pillow-like paper absorbing most of it as the bleeding slowed. Gently, he applied cream. But as the Old Man unpeeled a bandage from a translucent package, my mind slipped away. Something about the way he gently wrapped his hand around mine—almost like a hug—and squeezed made me remember. The Old Man's touch was fatherly and forgiving.

Then, all I could think about was the last night I heard my daughter sing.

•

The tennis ball that hung from the garage ceiling bounced on my windshield. Softly, the green fuzz popped up and down, making a dribbling sound. Like one of Pavlov's dogs, the instant the ball stopped, I was starving.

The automatic garage shuttered down. My jacket was around my shoulder when I swung open the door and gagged on the smell.

Instead of Wednesday night's chicken and potatoes, I smelled cigarettes.

The smoke stuck to the air like a malignant cancer. A harsh and ashy smell. The house was thick with it.

My elevated mood morphed to anger. Marla knew never to smoke in the house. Sammy was only seven and that type of secondhand smoke would wreak havoc on her development.

"Honey," I called out with some bite as I walked towards the kitchen. The smoke was getting thicker, stronger.

Silence.

"Marla!"

The smoke was now in my mouth, tainting my saliva and coating my nostrils. It fogged my vision as it got thicker and thicker. It wasn't just cigarettes, something was burning.

My heartrate increased as I moved. Catching a large breath of smoke, I coughed as I turned to the kitchen. My eyes stung.

Beyond a cloud of deep, black smoke, dinner veraciously boiled out of a pot. Water spouted and hissed off the sides. The flames cradled the underbelly of the pot like flickering, satanic hands. I pulled my collared shirt over my mouth, pushed the smoke away with one hand, and turned off the stove with the other. I slid open the window over the sink.

The contents of the pot quickly morphed from deadly concoction to calm liquid as the fingerlike flames dwindled. The way it transformed without the flames was startling. How anything so calm could become *so* dangerous so quickly and then go back to nothing again. One second liquid is cleaning, healing or hydrating, the next, it could be replacing the oxygen in your lungs as you drown. One second it keeps you alive, the next just the opposite. A simple, natural element that could determine whether you live or die. A decision that really isn't up to me or you.

Turning towards our breakfast table where I'd once spoon-fed our daughter as a newborn, was Marla, either asleep or dead. She slumped on the table next to an empty wine bottle, her deep, black hair over her face. A cigarette burned between her fingers. Ash sprinkled the table like innocent breadcrumbs.

With the smoke now quickly dissipating, I could see that Marla was breathing. Not dead. Asleep then. Her head lulled up and down in a gentle rhythm. So gentle in fact, it was as if she'd been asleep in our bed.

I was ready to tear her to pieces. Take the still burning tobacco and crush it in my naked hand. Untie the knot and let all of the strings run down into nothing.

But my Sammy. My precious, loving, caring, hopeful daughter. Marla was still the mother of that child. Something that—unfortunately—would never change.

I bolted up the stairs, listening for her. I caught the sound of her soft cries through a wooden door.

"Sammy!" I yelled out, "Sammy, sweetie! It's okay. I'm here. It's okay." I tossed her bedroom door open.

She wasn't there. Her room was neat as could be without a dress, blanket, or doll out of place. But the smell, the smell of burnt metal and ash stained every part of her room upstairs.

"Sammy!" I yelled again.

Through the wall beside me, I finally heard the sound of Sammy's cry. "Daddy! Daddy!"

The bathroom. Back out in the hallway, I saw that a towel had been scrunched beneath the door.

It took me a moment, but there she was. In a corner of the tub, shivering beside the damp curtain. Her teeth chattered. She was coming apart.

I reached for a towel as a plume of black smoke followed me into the room. She coughed, her small shoulders shaking as I wrapped the towel over her head and pulled her out in a shivering ball. The water was frigid, cutting.

"Why…why…is…it…so…cloudy?" She fought for the words between the ravaging chills. Her skin was prickled in goosebumps, her fingers nearly pruned to the bone.

With Sammy's teeny seven-year-old body sufficiently wrapped in a towel in my arms, I repeated again and again, "It's alright. I've got you. It's alright. I've got you."

Her crying gently slowed as she leaned further into me, tucking the top of her head just below my chin.

I carried her back to her room and closed the door behind us. She continued to shake. With each small moan, I tightened my hold on her, attempting to shoulder some of her pain, doing everything I could to just keep her warm.

She looked at me then through the lingering smoke in the room and what was left of the fading evening light. Her full blue eyes and soft, doughy cheeks, once vivacious, were now filled with fear. She had been caught on the hook of evil and betrayal. That look said more to me than any words could. It was the first time she'd realized—that I realized—I couldn't protect her. That no matter how much I loved her or how many safety nets I cast, nothing could keep her safe. That this world could gobble her up in an instant.

I kissed her forehead. "Get changed into your warm jammies," I said as I stood up. "I'll get your brush."

I walked out of her room without looking back. I closed the door, the smoke clearing out of the house, and sat down on the top of the stairs as I did everything I could to keep from falling to ash like the drifts from Marla's cigarette. My hands started to shake. I wasn't sure I'd ever forgive myself for leaving Sammy. How quickly things catch to flame.

I took a deep breath and steeled myself as I grabbed her hairbrush and opened the bathroom window to help clear out the rest of the smoke. When I returned to her room, Sammy was dressed in a set of frog-green pajamas, waiting for me at the edge of her bed.

Carefully, I took each lock of her golden-blond hair and brushed it straight, untangling every little knot, fray, and split. Sitting beside her, I gently brushed it all. Her wet hair slowly dried with each pass of the brush. A ritual she and I had been doing for years.

"No singing tonight, princess?"

I waited for a sound, a syllable or a note, but Sammy just kept looking straight forward. She hardly even flinched.

"Princess. Would you…"

"Why is Mommy sick all the time?" she blurted out.

I tried to focus on brushing her hair. Holding on to what I could and hoping to give her something to take what had happened off her mind.

"I know she's sick," she said. "I know because when it's all cloudy in the house, she…she coughs a lot. You don't know, Daddy, but I do. When you're not here, she coughs a lot."

I take one long lock at a time, focusing on each strand.

"Is Mommy going to die?"

I stopped brushing. I set my fingers below her chin

and turned her face gently to look at me. "Your mother is going to be just fine. She's not going to die, and everything is going to be okay. You don't need to worry, princess."

"But…but, Daddy?" Sammy began with some trepidation, "What…what if you're wrong?"

I was trapped in a place there was no escaping. No matter what I did, where I looked, I didn't have a choice. I was stuck in the sinking mud of my own creation.

This was my daughter; this was my life.

"If Mommy died, would she still be able…would she still be able to hear me sing?"

I took my hand and cradled it beside Sammy's cheek, brushing her face with my thumb. The look of uncertain hope on her face nearly broke me.

"One day, princess…one day the entire world is going to hear you sing."

Sammy lit back up and fell into my arms. It was a good thing, though, because I'd nearly lost what little strength I had left. Tears were now on the verge of pouring out of me.

As I went back to brushing her hair, that spark in her eyes that had been clouded by the fear and smoke returned and my Sammy began to sing. As always, the instant I heard her voice, my problems felt smaller. Her voice gently rose and fell as she carried a simple tune. One of her usual bedtime lullabies.

Following her every chord, my pain, exhaustion, and frustration lifted with her musical miasma. Carrying all of the bad somewhere far beyond.

Sammy repeated the melody. Somewhere in her song, I heard her passion and fire again. My daughter had rediscovered her own medicine that had so long helped heal her scars. A medicine, one day, I knew she would share with this dark world.

Once she was done, I pulled her covers back and kissed her on the forehead again.

"Sleep tight, princess."

Sammy smiled as I placed my hand over hers, and with all of her might, she squeezed as hard as she could. *Hugs for our hands*, she'd always called them.

But as I flicked off the light, I heard Sammy call out for me. Something she never did in the dark.

"Please, Daddy. Never leave me again."

•

The Old Man finished taping a bandage on my hand and poured himself more gin. "Some storm, eh."

It was coming down harder now. No longer falling in individual fragments but in blustering, large swaths. Like sheets of white. The snow was now blocking out the whole sky. As if nothing else existed beyond.

The Old Man was winded, I could tell. Apprehending the bartender must have taken more out of him than he'd expected. He was still catching his breath.

It was cold inside the cabin and my bad leg was

beginning to throb. I reached into my pocket for my prescription this time and washed it down with whiskey. I set the glass down. One final sip left.

"Usually in storms like this, our power gets bad, ya know. The two almost go hand in hand."

I didn't respond as I finished off the last sip and reached for the bottle. I filled my glass to the brim. My eyes went back out the window.

"So." The Old Man looked at me with sharp eyes. "Why do you drink?"

I'd come up with many lies over the years since the accident. Some of them were pretty good, good enough that sometimes I'd even get people to believe my story was something sweet. But something about watching the Old Man stand up for her made me want to tell him the hard truth. I don't know, maybe it had something to do with the fact that I was a little bit drunk, too, and couldn't muster up the energy for a lie. But even then, the truth was just as hard to talk about.

"Her real name isn't Squeeze," I began, "it's Samantha. Growing up, though, Marla, my ex-wife, we always just called her Sammy. All her friends at school did, too."

The Old Man adjusted his seat. It creaked loud enough to make me stop for a second before I continued.

"She had this fear of the dark when she was real young. Most kids do, of course, but she was also terrified when people talked to her when the lights were out. She would never let anyone say anything. So instead of saying goodnight, just before bed, I'd always put my hand over her, and she'd take both of her tiny hands and squeeze my hand as tight as she could. She called it *hugs for our hands*. Squeezing became her thing."

"That's precious, Don, really, ya know. So precious," the Old Man said with his cracked smile, but as he continued to look at me, he realized nothing about me was warm at that moment. Quickly, his mood dropped as he went even quieter than before.

I sighed as I looked out the window. The snow was really coming down.

"It was a night about six years ago. Marla and I had gotten into an argument. She almost set the house on fire, passed out drunk. Sammy wasn't safe with her anymore and I needed to do something, anything. So once Marla went to sleep, I packed all of Sammy's things in the car and just started driving. I had no idea where I was going. A hotel maybe, anywhere but there, near her.

"It was pouring rain. I was still mad. Sammy started to cry and told me she wanted to go back home, but I told her I was taking her somewhere better…somewhere safe. But even still, she was afraid. She could tell I wasn't thinking straight."

It was now completely silent in the parlor. The bartender had finished cleaning up the mess of glass and alcohol and disappeared somewhere in the middle of the Old Man bandaging the cuts on my hand. The storm had abated slightly, and tiny flakes kissed the windows. Even without any noise, it was all still a white ballet on display. There was no hiding.

The Old Man just listened now, sitting quietly, drinking his gin.

"The car I hit that night had an entire family inside. It was two days before Christmas. Husband. Wife. One son, two daughters. Eleven. Eight. And two. A perfectly happy, perfectly normal family. A family I now think about every stormy night... every...every night.

"I woke up Christmas Eve in the hospital with my leg busted in three places. I couldn't move I was in so much pain; they told me the other family was okay...but then...they told me about Sammy..."

The snow began to pick up, the winds did, too, the ballet becoming a maelstrom. The trees continued to hang over us. Waiting for their chance to spark fire.

"Sammy was in surgery when I woke up. I couldn't even walk to see her, so they rolled me to her room once she was out. But when I arrived that night, and I saw how swollen her head and face were...it broke me...it broke me like I couldn't believe. Her neck was in a brace and they shaved half her head for the surgery. Her gorgeous hair I'd been brushing her entire life was gone...She could barely open her eyes when they told me...when they told me that she'd never be able to speak again. That the injuries she'd suffered were to the portion of her brain related to speech...

"But when I rolled myself over to her side and I placed my hand over hers, even though she couldn't say anything, she knew to give my hand a hug. She squeezed it as hard as she could…and she always has ever since."

It was silent for some time after that as the Old Man and I just listened to the storm. Watching the windows pile with snow and the walls creak with the wind. The wood held firm for the most part, but we could tell the storm was growing stronger. Each second, more and more of the cabin shook.

"Leave my glass," I said to the Old Man. "I'm gonna check on her."

Pulling my bad leg out from under the table, I dragged it over to the staircase beside the bar. Using the handrails, I was able to pull myself up each individual step. At a rote pace, I climbed.

My fingers dug into the stained oak. My skin beneath my worn pants tensed with each pull. I felt all of it around me.

It was so cold now I could see my breath inside the cabin. To move at least warmed me up a bit.

The door to our room was ajar. It creaked as I did.

Squeeze sat in a rocking chair facing a blank wall, her knees pulled to her chest. Tears dribbled from her blue eyes.

"Everything alright?"

But she just kept rocking. Back and forth, her chair creaked beneath her.

"I just needed some adult time. I told you I wouldn't be long."

It's hard to understand her if you're not used to it, but I'd spent so much time around my daughter since the accident that I was one of the few people who could. Through groans, she knew she'd be able to get her point across to me.

I was all alone. She mumbled.

"I know you were," I began, now by her side. "But you were okay, weren't you? I knew you would be. I wouldn't have left if I didn't think you'd be okay."

You lied. You said you'd never leave me alone.

"I didn't lie, I was just downstairs. Right out at the table."

I don't feel good. My head hurts.

"I'm sure you just need rest, princess. More rest."

Letting her guard down a bit, she slumped her shoulders. She looked tired.

Can I come down and sit with you?

"It's late," I began. "Here, let's get you ready for bed."

Now that she was able to bathe herself, I laid her clean pajamas and towel out on the countertop and waited on the other side of the bathroom door just in case. She'd told me that it made her feel more comfortable to know if she needed help, I wasn't far away.

Afterwards, as always, I grabbed her brush and combed her hair.

Sitting beside her on the bed, I took her long, golden curls in my hands. With careful attention, I ran the brush through it all. One hand was holding her hair, the other brushing it smooth.

But ever since the accident, every time I brushed her hair, I was reminded of that night. Through the parts in her hair, I could see the long scars from all the procedures that lined her scalp. Pink, fleshy skin. As I brushed, each of the suture marks stared back at me.

The other difference between now and then was she used to be able to sing—sharing with me the latest hymn she'd been mastering—while now she could only hum.

With her lips closed, she hummed away. The noise crackled through her throat and attempted to carry a tune. Despite getting lost here and there, she continued to try. Doing her best to make music.

Somewhere inside was her angelic choir voice. Trapped beneath the scars I couldn't see. Broken and battered, yet still attempting to escape. Searching for alternate routes out of the rubble.

For years, I continued to believe that one day her voice would find its way out from under the destruction. That if she kept trying, she'd finally strike a note that would prove to her she could do it again. The one glimmer of light we all needed but never quite happened. I guess I'd given up on that now.

I wanted to clap once she was done, tell her how good she was or request another, but to hear the pain only broke me more. It served as an auditory reminder that when my daughter had needed me most, I couldn't protect her.

Once I was done combing her hair, Squeeze slipped into bed.

"Goodnight, princess." I said while turning down the lamp.

Then, as we did every night, I reached my hand out over her and she squeezed it. As hard as she could. Which, at one point—during our darkest months—was the only way she'd been able to let me know she was okay, at one point the only way we could communicate at all.

I dragged myself into the bathroom and stared right at myself in the mirror. Attempting to slow everything down.

My leg was starting to hurt real bad, so I rubbed it up and down on both sides of my knee. Through the outside of my pants, I pressed on it, then leaned only on my good one to take some of the pressure off.

When I opened the bathroom door, I could hear Squeeze was asleep. Her nighttime coo was already in full rhythm. Her long, blond hair rested over her shoulder and pillow.

The Old Man handed me my drink once I arrived back downstairs.

"She doin' alright?"

I fell into my seat.

"Yeah."

"Ya know, if I may add just one more thing," he started after just a moment.

I didn't say anything.

The Old Man continued, "I hope you know how lucky you are to have your...Squeeze. She may be different, bud, but I know me, and my love would've done anything to have someone like her. I promise that to be true."

Sometime after that, the Old Man got up and left

while I kept on drinking.

I'd wondered then what any decent man would do in my circumstance. What the noble path was as well as the not-so-noble. How much I needed the freedom, yet how responsible I was. How what was waiting for me ahead made me feel and how much protection I could offer. I hadn't settled anywhere.

If it is acting not out of love, then what?

Suddenly, the front door flew open so violently it nearly tore out of the jam. It slapped the back wall again and again and again. Cold air and snow screamed into the cabin.

Twisting around in my chair, I realized that nobody was around at all. It was just me in the parlor.

Like hell, I pushed myself out of my seat and went for the door. This was not gentle mother nature, this was a white hurricane, throwing blocks of sleet like thick dust. I felt my face suck back with the bite of the cold. I could hardly keep up straight.

Trying for the door, I lost my balance and slid to the floor. I'd nearly broken my fall with my face.

Using my good leg, I angled it into the crook of the door to try and kick it shut. I kept pushing and pushing from the floor until, eventually, I was able to get it closed.

Lying on my back, I breathed heavily, realizing how loud I'd been. My chest pumped hard.

Then the lights—all of them—snapped off.

I was staring straight at the ceiling of the parlor when it went completely dark. In the black, I could feel the snow hitting the walls, cutting at the windows. Everything started to shut down.

My leg was now hurting so badly I just kept lying there. I had no desire to move.

But, like a hole in the earth, I felt an emptiness pulling me down. Sucking on my skin like leeches and picking at my flesh like vultures. One by one, taking every part of me deeper into the darkness. I was slowly becoming ashes. I guess we all do.

I jolted up as if it had all been a bad dream. The air was turning icy and bitter. With the power out, the temperature had started dropping quickly.

My eyes had adjusted to the dark, but not well enough for me to move with much confidence. I was walking mostly by feeling with my hands. I could feel the cold now in my bones. Any exposed skin stung; my teeth chattered.

I slipped on the first stair, misplacing my bad leg. Grasping for something to grab hold of, the cuts on my hand reopened. Warm blood began to run off my wrist.

Reaching for the railing again, my bloodied hand only made it slicker.

My chest and face were now frozen. I was trying to both close off my body to the cold and open my gait in order to walk, the deep challenge of moving in this darkness and cold.

A flashlight shone over my face. The Old Man stood over me from the upstairs hall.

"Jesus, Don. You alright?"

He helped me to my feet, but even feeling his hand I

could tell he, too, was freezing.

"Damn thing's busted from the storm," he wheezed between shivers. "I'll go wake the boy to see if he can have a look."

I was so drunk, cold, and tired I could hardly think. Every movement was a struggle and every thought an inconvenience.

I limped into our room and went for the bathroom first. In the thin moonlight that made it through the storm, I placed my shivering hand into the sink to rinse off the newly opened wounds, but when I went to turn on the faucet, nothing came out. My warm blood turned cold as it ran all over the porcelain.

Wrapping the cuts in a hand towel, my shivering had only grown more violent.

The bathroom was somehow warmer than our bedroom. Squeeze was still asleep in the same spot I'd left her.

Cocooned in her blanket, her calm face brought me ease. Her long hair flowed over the pillow. But despite her restful appearance, the storm erupted once more. This time so violently that the entire cabin shook. The drapes, blankets, and even walls danced a sort of turning sway. My balance felt uneasy.

Still shivering beyond the point of fluid movement, I limped to be right beside her. Putting my hand over hers, I could feel she was freezing.

I pulled all of the extra blankets off the chairs, sofas, and mantels around our room and laid them over her, tucking them tight with each new layer.

I still worried it wouldn't be enough. The cold that was taking over the blacked-out cabin was enough now to suck the air out of my lungs.

Searching for more blankets, I ripped apart our room. Drawers and drawers were pulled out of sockets to land onto the floor.

What's going on? She asked in a frightened mumble.

"Bad storm, princess."

Now settling on wool jackets and shirts, I tossed anything that looked warm over my daughter in the hopes of protecting her. Of giving her some cushion from this cold.

I looked again at her restful face as the storm continued to howl.

"How's that, princess? Warmer?"

She nodded slightly then continued to lie still beneath all of the blankets and shreds of clothing I could scrape together.

But then, I saw that same look in her eyes once more. The one that had stayed with me all of these years. A look of fear and betrayal. Ice-blue eyes that wanted to scream at me but couldn't.

My eyes then joined in on shivering. Slowly pooling with cold tears, my vision of my daughter blurred. I was already freezing, but still, somehow, I got colder.

"I'm sorry," I cried out. "Princess…I'm so sorry."

I fell to my knees on the floor at her bedside. My head collapsed onto the bed right before her.

With my blood-soaked hand, I took hold of her delicate palm. The once soft-white hand towel was now hot-red.

But instead of squeezing my hand in a hug, she did nothing. I felt nothing of the sort. No feeling of her fingers wrapping around mine. No rubbing of her palm. No curling or arching of her wrist. My hand laid limp in hers as she just continued to look right at me. No sign of her forgiveness or love. No communication other than that look. She wanted nothing to do with me any longer.

With my daughter's limp hand in mine, her hand was now the coldest thing in the room.

"I'm so sorry," I said again, trailing off. "I'm so sorry, Squeeze…"

My shivers made it more difficult to move, but I got up and limped back towards the door. I did so without looking back. I didn't even say goodbye.

I wanted to cry out or scream, tell her I was sorry again, listen to her sing, but I was too cold. I couldn't do anything more than just struggle towards the end.

From the top of the stairs, I could hear the front door torn open again, slapping the wall. Wind was howling alongside the snow. No one was in the parlor.

Doing my best not to fall down the stairs, I slid off of each one to the next. My bloodied hand held on to the wooden railing. My bad leg felt as though it was about to split.

The door continued to slap the wall. Snow had begun to pile in the doorway. Like tiny knives, the flakes pricked my cheeks.

I got to the doorway and just stopped.

A blinding sheet of white blustered before me. With snow coming down now so fiercely, I couldn't see inches before my eyes. Like I was standing at the edge of the world.

I was disoriented and afraid. I was shaking. My hand bled; my bad leg throbbed.

I fell to my knees.

All she ever wanted was to sing. To make undying music that could deliver gladness to the world. Only to be stricken down. In a violent storm and in the presence of the one person who had failed her time and time again. No one was watching but me.

In a fury of anger, I went through it all.

"You're not real!" I screamed as loud as I could at the wind. "You're a damn coward!"

I was letting it all fall down. I had nothing left.

"Show yourself!" My eyes started to water and tear. "Show yourself, then…please. I'm begging you to make it stop…"

Looking out into the darkness, I waited. I wasn't sure what I was expecting to happen, but the winds kept coming. Snow kept blistering my skin. My hand kept bleeding. My daughter still couldn't sing. There wasn't anyone listening.

I rose to my feet.

"Fine," I said while wiping my face. "I'll go on anyway."

I began to cry. Weeping while the storm increased its rage. My hand continued to dribble as a mixture of blood and tears stained the snow. A violent color.

The snow began to collect over me. I could feel the pain slowly starting to go away. I could feel it all starting to go away.

As terrible as it was, I was with her then. My fears and anguish all but left. My biting pain, gone.

But somewhere up ahead, further beyond the point I couldn't see, something started pulling me. As if I had needed to go there all along.

Pulling my bad leg along, I limped into the storm. Howling winds and stabbing cold suddenly felt less painful. There was less of any of it going on around me. A sort of quiet peace.

It was the storm, the wind and the tall match-like trees. I was small compared to it. We all are.

I turned to look again, but by now I couldn't even see the cabin. Without it now as a landmark, I had no idea where I was. Up, down, right or left were all a guess. As if caught in a rumbling avalanche. The cold kept on coming and the wind was an evil, mocking laugh.

I started to feel an upward slope beneath my feet. I was coming towards maybe some sort of hill.

But instead of feeling cold, scared, angry or sad, I felt fresh. I felt awake, and I felt like things might just be alright.

My feet stopped just before a sharp cliff, my toe brushing the edge. Looking up then, the snow began to slow. The wind gently toned down and the blinding darkness eased. All of a sudden, and in an instant, it was clear as a summer morning.

The natural order of things resumed just as easily as they'd been derailed. And suddenly, I was not trapped in this frozen hell, but a wintry dreamscape.

Soft snow padded the hillside; the cold air became manageable. It was gorgeous.

A long running waterfall came out from the clouds. It ran over circular rocks, snow-covered bushes and a gentle ravine below. The face of the cliff glimmered in the clearing. Trees stood everywhere with caught snow.

I began to imagine the Old Man and his wife here. The many springs and summers they'd probably spent splashing in this water. All the times they'd talked. Through their entire lives, I felt like I was watching them fall in love.

I'd never know her name, and not even his, but somehow that didn't feel important. Because now, here, and in this moment, I was watching them. I was watching the Old Man as a smitten young man, courting the girl of his dreams. There was no *here* without *her*.

Then, from that open sky, I heard voices. Initially, through the storm, I wasn't sure if I could believe if they were real or not, but in this calm air, there they were. There was no doubting their song.

They reminded me of Squeeze. Her life and her vibrance. Of the beauty of simplicity.

Just as quickly as this moment arrived, it passed. The storm came roaring back—more vicious than before.

I kept listening for the voices through the cold wind. A loud crack sounded.

I felt it over me. Another thunderous crack sounded deep into the thicket. A wind was what I felt first, until the falling feeling came right over me.

But instead of only being able to hear her then, I could now see her. I was looking right at her flawless face, remembering all the times I'd seen her smile. Her long hair that looked like a halo. All the times I'd held her, kissed her forehead, listened to her song. Her face then was every memory all at once. Her whole life, which had been all the best parts of mine.

I was surrounded by it. The high-pitched tune was being carried out. And as the voices carried around me, just as you thought they'd run out of breath, they continued.

I couldn't feel, taste, touch or move. But I could listen. I could hear them, all of them. Their voices rolling towards me in a wave.

Then I realized I was without pain. I had no more regret, no more sorrow or anguish. I couldn't feel much still, but I was lighter.

Something was carrying me as the voices continued.

I kept blinking my eyes, but all was white. Tiny pockets of white kept falling down. I saw them fly by.

I should have been more afraid, but something wasn't allowing me to be. As if such thoughts were an impossible waste.

All I knew and could feel were those voices of song.

Portending simplistic beauty, not burden. Striking elementary notes that together in unison were magnificent. And as each voice of magic got stronger, more of the white continued to fall. More of it gathered around me.

We are all stuck. Stuck in our routine, focus or trade. Carried away in a plan that most likely will not happen. Thinking about everything other than what is right before our hands. Endlessly avoiding the beauty in being lost.

We only believe what we can see when what we can see is but a fraction of all life's beauty. Gorgeous miracles happen every second when we'd prefer to stick to our plan, to refrain from getting lost. Our habits become our religion. We study for success, happiness, fame and worship those who have it. We pray for the universe to conspire in our favor.

I am like you. I played, I worked, I loved, and I died. I desired nice things and was upset when I didn't get them. I complained. I felt guilt and harbored regret.

But in the end, all I heard was her song. The absolute brilliance in something so delicate. The voice I'd hoped one day I may hear again.

It was her voice as I'd always remembered it could be. Smooth like bare feet in an orchard. Floating through an endless expanse of golden fruit.

Being carried to my ending by her sound once more. With the white around me no longer cold, but warm.

ACKNOWLEDGMENTS

Every project takes a village, and I consider myself beyond fortunate that these talented individuals are a part of mine. A special thank you to my editor Christine Nielson, your sharp eye and key additions to this piece were seamless. Thank you for taking my disorganized ramblings and turning them into a story. Nuno Moreira, thank you for building the perfect home for these characters. As far as artists go, you are one of the best. A quick thanks to my bud Alex Hart, thank you for all the help ya know. Another thanks to Judi Weiss for offering final eyes on this work. And finally, a massive thank you to my editor, manager, and best friend Chris Varonos. Thank you for all of your notes, ideas and suggestions as we brought this thing together. You're the most talented storyteller I know. Christine, Nuno, X, Judi, Chris, you all are what make Summer House a family. All of you have my whole heart.

"The novel wins by points, the short story wins by knockout."
- Julian Cortazar

Summer House Shorts is a platform created to allow authors the opportunity to peel back the rules. To experiment, take risks, sharpen style, or augment a voice. Shorts can contain a slice of life, an inward look, a distant memory, or an entire lifetime. With quick hitting writing, shorts can be taken in one sitting, yet utilize the power of prose to move, inspire, challenge, or perhaps suggest new ideas on how to live. Summer House Shorts are one of the many ways we package the art of story.

ABOUT THE AUTHOR

JD Slajchert is an American novelist who was born and raised in Southern California. He wrote his debut novel, *MoonFlower*, during his final two years as a student-athlete at the University of California, Santa Barbara. When tragedy struck and he lost his biggest fan Luc Bodden to Sickle Cell Disease, he knew he needed to preserve Luc's spirit and honor his memory by writing his first book. Following his many trips to Mammoth Lakes, California, he became moved to write his first purely fiction work, "Joining the Choir Invisible." He credits much of his inspiration to many of the authors from the lauded Lost Generation, and has aspirations of one day living in Paris. He is currently working on his second novel.

For more information about JD Slajchert, please visit his personal website: www.jdwritesbooks.com